THIS BOOK BELONGS TO:

THE PERFECT POTTY ZOO

The Funniest **ABC** Book

Author
Agnes Green

Animals from A to Z are very much like you,
They play, they eat, they sleep, they dream,
They even pee and poo!

And every one, in their own way,
has chosen for their home,
the perfect potty, Just for them,
to be their potty throne.

So, while you sit upon your seat,
and do what you must do,
listen to the stories of the Perfect Potty Zoo

Albert Alligator loves to sing a little song,
as he sits upon his potty, he knows it won't take long.
Just a little while later he will go outside and play.
Would you like to sing like Albert, as you sit here today?

B Betty Bunny Rabbit has a habit every night,
of sitting on her potty, before mom turns off the light.
She'll sleep happy and so comfy, snuggled up the whole night through,
'cause she sat upon her potty, before bedtime, just like you.

A Cat named Calvin Cunningham is healthy as can be,
Whenever he goes potty, if he poos or if he pees,
Calvin cleans his paws and whiskers, and his face and tail and fur,
That keeps Calvin very healthy, so he's happy and he purrs.

Dillon and Demetri, the darling Duckling twins,
have races on their potties. They love to see who wins.
Though sister Donna Ducking tells them not to rush,
the twins just will not listen, they tell her she should hush.

Emma is an Emu and has legs so very tall.
While she sits upon her potty, she can bounce a basketball!
Her potty is real high, so she doesn't have to stoop.
Whenever she goes potty, when she needs to pee or poop.

F

Freddie the Flamingo has a potty that is pink.
When he sits upon it, he rests and reads and thinks.
In fact, he finds his potty a rather pleasant spot.
Do you agree with Freddie? I don't see why not.

Gwendolyn Gorilla is an active two-year-old.
She loves to swing from branches and rarely does what she is told.
She doesn't like to use her potty. She would rather climb and play.
Her mom says, "She's not ready, and, for now, that is okay."

Now Harry Hippopotamus goes potty every day.
When arriving home from preschool, before going out to play,
Just because he is a hippo in the middle of a zoo.
Harry's really not that different, he goes potty just like you.

When Ignatius Iguana chose a potty for himself,
he went shopping with his Papa, and looked over every shelf.
There were blue ones, there were pink ones, but the one that he liked best
was a camo-colored potty. It blended in among the rest.

Little Jimmy Jo the Jackal, his two brothers and his sis,
chose a real tall-sided potty. With one like that, they couldn't miss!
It was perfect for the Jackals, who found it easier to pee,
and make it in the potty, not on the floor accidentally.

Kimberly Koala is a sweet and quiet bear.
She has a lime green potty to match the ribbons in her hair.
When she chews on eucalyptus or she climbs in the bamboo,
Kimberly Koala keeps her potty well in view.

Lily Anna Lemur has a long and stripped tail.
Sometimes when she goes potty, she starts to cry and wail,
For her tail it is so pretty, but it can get in the way.
So she must be very careful when she potties every day.

A monkey named Montana was a silly, playful guy.
He never used his potty and his momma asked him why.
He didn't really answer, and placed his potty on his head,
Then he danced around the playroom, and he jumped upon his bed.

Nolan Brown the Numbat, from Australia's Western side
has stripes upon his fur, which are there to help him hide,
while he eats his favorite sandwiches of termites, sand, and ants.
Then he sits down on his potty, and when he's done, pulls up his pants.

Octavia Rose Octopus doesn't have a single care.
As she sits upon her potty, she has many legs to spare.
She can hold the toilet paper and a book or two,
She can even paint a picture when she pees and when she poos.

Patty Paula Platypus had a constant worry
of what to do if she should need a potty in a hurry.
Her momma told her not to fret, it would be okay,
just take a break from time to time, to try throughout the day.

Quinton the Quokka has a potty by his bed,
with pink and purple polkadots and tiny stripes of red.
He decorated it himself with stickers and with glue.
Maybe you would like to decorate your potty too.

R Whenever Roscoe Ringtail, the rascally raccoon camps out in the forest underneath the moon, he takes his potty with him. Roscoe is prepared, in case he needs his potty, out in the open air.

Have you heard of Sammy Seal? He is a clever guy.
He can do some awesome tricks that you might like to try,
Like singing while he balances a ball upon his nose,
Sitting on his potty and playing piano with his toes.

Tiffany the Tortoise is slow as slow can be,
even on the potty when she poos and when she pees.
Tiffany explained to me, she doesn't have to hurry,
Eventually she'll get there... There is no need to worry!

Andrea the Urial is a sheep that's wild and sweet,
with curly horns upon her head and grass beneath her feet.
She has a pretty potty that she sprays with nice perfume,
so it smells like fields of flowers when it sits there in her room.

V

Three Vultures by the name of Vince all went to the same school.
One went by Vincent, one by Vince, the third by Vinnie Cool.
The three were the best of friends, you see, and went about together,
even to the potty. They were true birds of a feather.

W

William Wiggins Walrus was a happy little guy.
He loved to fly his kite, way up in the sky.
His papa even told him that as an extra special treat,
he could fly his favorite kite while on his potty seat.

Have you heard of Xander Xenarthra and his cousin Bobbie Sue?
They were playing hide and seek once, at the playground in the zoo
when it happened without warning... Xander really had to go,
so they ran to find a potty, but alas, they were too slow.

If ever you bump into a Yak named Emmy Lou
while she's walking through the grocery store or playing peekaboo,
ask her about her perfect potty, and she'll sit a while to rest,
and tell you about the potty, which she prefers the best.

Zelda Zebra, just the other day, went galloping to town,
She was wearing her best sundress and a gold and diamond crown.
When she had to use the potty, she didn't have to double back,
For she has hers with her always, in a green and purple sack.

Now you see that all the animals are very much like you.
One and all from A to Z, when they pee and when they poo,
has a potty that is perfect at the Perfect Potty Zoo.
But, now potty time is over. You've done great! Let's shout hurray!
Pull up your pants and wash your hands... It's time to go outside and play!

THe End

FOLLOW Me!

PLEASE...

PLEA Zzz

PLEASE, LEAVE A REVIEW!

I hope you enjoyed this cute little story!

Reviews from awesome customers like you

help others to feel confident

about choosing this book too.

Please take a minute to share your experience!

I will be forever grateful.

Yours, Agnes Green

THANK YOU!

"It's time for bed... Hip hip hooray! Let's all give a cheer!
The day is through. We've had such fun. Now sleepy time draws near.

Before you drift away to dream, let's check in at the zoo.
I hear they're having a parade and a pajama party too!"

Don't miss another book of mine!
"Today I'm a Monster"

Made in the USA
Lexington, KY
10 June 2018